Knowledge and Power

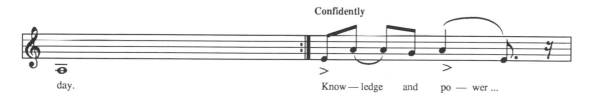

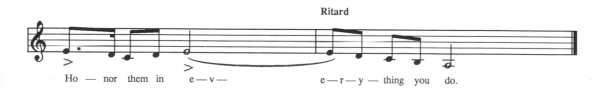

Naro, the Ancient Spider

The Creation of the Universe

Story and music by
Susan Joyce
Illustrations by
D. C. DuBosque

Inspired by an ancient Oceanic
Creation Myth

Peel Productions
Molalla, Oregon

*For Leah, who will always be part
of my universe.*
—SJ

*For Paulette and Mike, a wonderful source
of support and inspiration!*
—DD

Text and music copyright
© 1989 Susan Joyce DuBosque
Illustrations copyright
©1990 D. C. DuBosque

Available soon as a
school musical
production.

First Edition
January 1991

5 4 3 2 1

This book's illustrations were done
with pastels and colored pencils.
Design by the illustrator using an Apple
Macintosh computer and PageMaker software,
with laser proofs generously donated by
Hot Off The Press, Inc.
Text typeface is Cheltenham; cover is Goudy.
Museum-quality color separations, printing and
binding by Hindy's Enterprise, Ltd., Hong Kong.
Near-fanatical attention to details by Yoh Jinno of
Jinno International, Chestnut Ridge, New York.

Library of Congress Cataloging-in-Publication Data

Joyce, Susan, 1945-
    Naro, the Ancient Spider : the creation of the universe / story
and music by Susan Joyce ; illustrations by D.C. DuBosque.
        p.   cm.
        "Myths of the heavens."
        "Inspired by an ancient Oceanic creation myth."
        Summary: describes how the world was created by Naro the
Ancient Spider, and her son Naro the Younger.
        ISBN 0-939217-04-X (hard cover) : $12.00
        1. Creation--folklore. [1. Folklore--Oceania.] I. DuBosque,
D.C., ill. II. Title.
        PZ8.1.J79NAR 1991
        398.24'52544'0995 - - dc20   90-14156

In the beginning, there was no man, no woman, no animal, no bird, no tree, no insect, no earth and no sky. There was no night and no day. There was no spring or summer. No winter or fall. There was only the great ocean of life and Naro the Ancient Spider. High above the ocean of life, in the web of the heavens, she sat alone — in emptiness and darkness.

After timeless ages had passed, Naro the Ancient became restless and began to weave. She pulled thin, strong threads of silk through her spinnerets and wove until she became not one Naro, but two: Naro the Ancient and her son, Naro the Younger. When the weaving was done Naro the Ancient smiled. Then she sat and rested, stroking her jaws, while Naro the Younger waited quietly close by.

Finally she spoke. "Son, my work is almost complete," she said, caressing her jaws and curved fangs with her feelers. "I will leave you soon. But, before I go I will create a universe — a place for you to play and practice the gifts of knowledge and power I will leave with you."

Naro the Younger watched with wonder as Naro the Ancient stood. Streamers of light shimmered from her as she braced her front legs and cupped her slender feelers into the shape of an open sea shell. She took a long, deep breath and in a steady voice began to chant.

"Oieee–ah–ou–hoi…."

The sound shook the web of the heavens. Beams of red, gold and blue crowned the darkness with radiant light.

"Oieee–ah–ou–hoi…."

She chanted again and again until the emptiness was filled with the beautiful vibrating sound of

"Oieee–ah–ou–hoi…."

In the center of the sound Naro the Ancient stood rhythmically rubbing her feelers together. Sparks flew. Torrents of light flowed from her long legs like lava and plummeted down into the great ocean of life. Naro the Younger's eyes grew wide as he watched a steaming planet be born far below.

"Oieee–ah," he cried out. "It's beautiful!"

Naro the Ancient bowed.

Then, rising, she placed her warm feelers on Naro the Younger's head. She swayed, back and forth and forth and back, singing:

*"Knowledge and power
are gifts I give to you.
Honor them and use them well
in all...you say and do.
The universe — a place to play, a place
to practice your gifts every day.
Knowledge and power are gifts I give to you.
Honor them and use them well
in everything you do.
The universe — a place to play, a place
to practice your gifts every day.
Knowledge and power....
Honor them in everything you do."*

When her song was finished, Naro the Ancient continued to sway, back and forth and forth and back, drumming lightly on the web of the heavens until the new planet had cooled and settled. In the hush that followed she rubbed her feelers together once more.

Sparks flew. Light flowed from the Ancient Spider's body until she was encircled by a fiery golden glow. Naro the Younger gazed in awe as the light grew then dimmed, growing fainter and fainter, and fainter, until the Ancient Spider vanished from sight.

Naro the Younger sat quietly, in the stillness of the web of the heavens, and studied the new born planet bobbing in the great ocean of life below.

"...a place to play, a place to practice your gifts every day?" he questioned.

"And, how do I enter the planet?" he asked puzzled. With a jump, he dropped down and began to examine the sky of the planet.

"There must be an opening somewhere," he said. He skittered back and forth and forth and back, searching everywhere for a crack or a hole in the pale blue sky. But it was seamless as far as he could see.

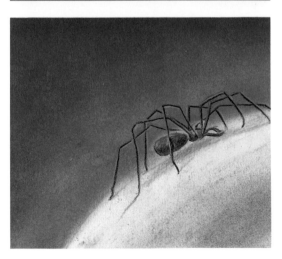

"The earth and sky have not been separated," he said exasperated. Frantically, he called to his mother. "Ancient One. Can you hear me? M–m–mother? Are you there?"

There was no answer and no sign of the Ancient Spider.

Exhausted, Naro the Younger lay down on the top of the sky.

He fell into a deep slumber and while he slept he dreamed of the gifts of knowledge and power the Ancient One had given him. When he was rested, he awakened.

"Power," he said stretching. "I have power."

He thumped his thick chest with one leg, then knelt and began to probe impatiently, drumming on the sky.

But nothing happened. He curled, then uncurled, his feelers and drummed again. Still nothing happened.

"I will use all my power." Naro the Younger announced, drumming a third time with all eight legs.

He watched and waited, rocking back and forth and forth and back.

Suddenly, before him, a small opening appeared.

"Aaaah," Naro murmured. He peeked through the narrow hole. All was dark and he could see nothing.

"Ahlo," he shouted into the hole.

"Ah–lo–lo–lo–lo–lo…," the hole replied.

"Ahh–ha," Naro exclaimed with delight.

"Ah–h–h–ha–ha–ha–ha," the hole echoed.

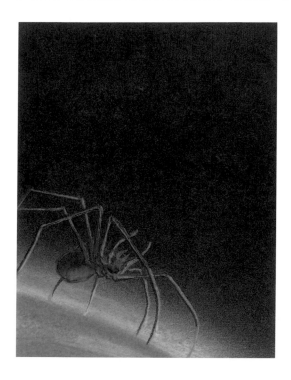

He chanted again and again until all was filled with the beautiful vibrating sound of
"Oieee–ah–ou–hoi…."

He rubbed his feelers together until two sparklets of light ignited. Together they formed a little luminous moth. Naro giggled.

"Oieee–ah," he said dancing about. "My first creation."

Naro stood and carefully braced his front legs, cupping his feelers into the shape of an open sea shell. He took a long deep breath and in a small, shaky voice he chanted,
"Oieee–ah–ou–hoi…."

The sound gently swayed the web of the heavens.
"Oieee–ah–ou–hoi…."

"Go through the hole," Naro said to the luminous moth, "and tell me what is there. With the light from your body you will be able to see through darkness," he explained.

The moth flitted and fluttered about, as if she didn't understand.

"Oh please," Naro pleaded.

The moth spread her wings and flew in a small figure eight, then disappeared into the blackness below.

Naro sat, rocking back and forth and forth and back, and waited and waited for her return.

With a sparkle of light, the moth appeared.

"Creatures," she said, shuddering. "They lie sleeping in the dark."

"Show me," Naro instructed. "Please, lead the way with your light, little moth."

With the flickering of the moth lighting the way, they dropped to the place where giant turtles lay sleeping.

"Turtles!" Naro called to them. "Awake!"

There was silence as the sleeping turtles lay lifeless.

"Move!" Naro instructed, drumming on the turtles' shells.

The giant turtles slowly begin to moan and move.

"Stand!" commanded Naro, lifting his front legs. "Stand up, and lift the sky!"

Clawing and clattering, the turtles stood.

"Higher," he demanded.

The turtles lifted their heads and stood on their hind legs.

They pushed and pushed with all their might but the sky moved no higher.

"Rest," he said to the turtles. With a thump they fell to the ground.

Naro was discouraged. He sat down to think. But, instead, he fell fast asleep and again he dreamed of the gifts of knowledge and power the Ancient Spider had left with him. He dreamed of the great ocean of life below. And, he dreamed of a conger — a mighty eel who ruled the deep blue sea. When he was rested, he awakened.

"Knowledge," he whispered, stroking his jaws. "The knowledge of the heavens is mine." He drummed his chest softly.

Then Naro stood and stretched each of his long legs. He took a deep breath and called to the mighty conger.

"Mighty Conger, Lord of the deep sea!
The earth and sky need separating.
Can you please help me?
Mighty Conger, Lord of the deep sea!
The earth and sky need separating.
Can you set them free?"

The great ocean of life began to sway. Small ripples of silver chased each other into gentle rolling waves. Swirling and twirling, the waters churned higher.

Then a great surge of foam splashed upward, tossing the planet to and fro. A pillow of white appeared carrying the mighty conger — Lord of the deep sea.

The waves parted and quieted. In a deep, husky voice the conger answered the call of Naro.

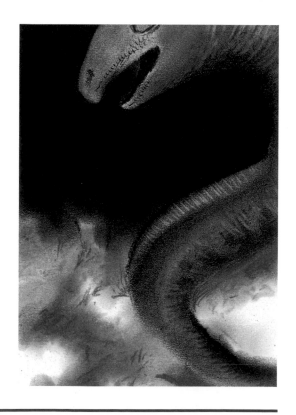

"I am Conger, Lord of the deep sea.
The earth and sky need separating.
I can set them free
I am Conger, Lord of the deep sea.
The earth and sky need separating.
The sea will set them free."

"The heavens bless you,"
Naro said, bowing.

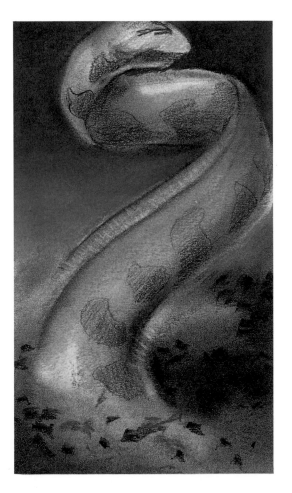

Then the Conger slipped into the space between the earth and sky. Uncoiling his huge body he pressed upward with his head until the earth rumbled and the sky shook. The deep blue waters of the sea rushed in behind him, raising the sky higher. As the waves pushed, the great ocean of life ripped the roots of the sky and separated it from the land below. The earth sank deeper, under the pressure of the Conger's great tail, and the shimmering sea flooded in.

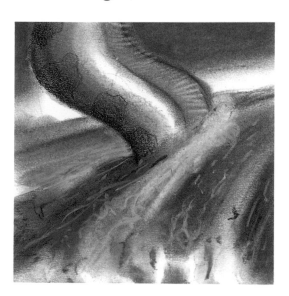

Naro rejoiced and the earth and sky joined him in praise,

"Mighty Conger!
Lord of the deep sea!
You shook the earth
and moved the sky.
You have set them free.
Mighty Conger!
Lord of the deep sea!
The earth and sky
give thanks to you
and to the great sea."

The great ocean of life began to sway gently and snuggle down to rest in the crevices between the earth and the sky. Small ripples of silver gathered into gentle rolling waves and carried the mighty Conger home to rest in the deepest blue of the great Ocean of Life.

Naro was pleased. "O–ieee," he said, rocking back and forth and forth and back — admiring the way the earth and sea fit smoothly together.

Then Naro noticed that the sky was without sides. "The sky must have sides." he said. "I shall attach the sky to the earth." He leaped up and began pulling down the edges of the sky. He tied knots here and there, and there and here, until it was fastened all around to the earth below.

"O–ieee–ah! It's beautiful!" He boasted.

Suddenly the sky blackened and the earth was covered with a giant shadow. Naro looked in all directions and began to move forward, cautiously, one step at a time. When he saw the body of the shadow, he leapt across the earth. Pouncing on it, he thrust his fangs into the giant body, crushing it. With a thud the shadow fell.

Naro knelt to examine it. "Oieee, noooo," he gasped. "I have slain the Ancient One." Weeping, he gently embraced the hairy body that had been the Ancient Spider.

"Oh Ancient One — creator of light," he whispered, gazing in awe, "you will always be part of the universe."

He gently plucked an eye from the Ancient Spider's head and flung it high into the web of the heavens, to the east.

"The Sun," Naro proclaimed, "will light our way by day."

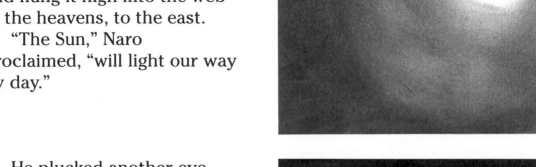

He plucked another eye from the Ancient One and threw it west, high into the web of the heavens.

"The Moon," Naro said softly "will brighten all our nights."

Naro then gathered the remaining eyes and the small fragments of the Ancient Spider's scattered body. He hurled them high into the web of the heavens, where they became stars too numerous to count and too many to name.

Streamers of light
shimmered from him as Naro
braced his front legs and
cupped his slender feelers into
the shape of an open sea shell.
He took a long, deep breath
and in a steady voice, he sang:

The Ancient spider's eyes will shine —
the sun by day, the moon by night.
The Ancient spider's eyes
will fill the world with light.
The sun will warm the earth by day,
from dawn till dusk to light the way.
The sun, the sun, the sun —
will fill the world with light.

The Ancient spider's eyes will shine —
the sun by day, the moon by night.
The Ancient spider's eyes
will fill the world with light.
The moon by night will light the sky,
from dusk till dawn will shine on high.
The moon, the moon, the moon —
will fill the world with light.

"My work is almost complete," Naro said, caressing his jaws and curved fangs with his feelers. "But, before I go I will create caretakers — people to care for this beautiful universe."

Naro knelt in the soft earth and began to dig a deep hole. As he dug, he chanted:

"Oieee–ah–ou–hoi…."
"Oieee–ah–ou–hoi…."
until the web of the heavens swayed with the soothing sound of
"Oieee–ah–ou–hoi…."

When he had reached the core of the earth, Naro took the powerful jaws and fangs of the Ancient Spider and placed them in the moist dirt. "The tree of life." he proclaimed.

Naro covered them with the rich, red soil and packed the earth all around.

Then he sat and waited. Rocking back and forth and forth and back, he watched and waited, and waited and watched, until a small green shoot appeared. The shoot grew taller and stronger until a tree was formed.

The tree grew, taller and stronger and stronger and taller, until flowers blossomed on its limbs. As the lush petals fell they bounced to life as blue–eyed, red–skinned people.

"O–ieee! You are beautiful," he exclaimed.

The red–skinned people laughed, then stretched and reached for the light blue sky.

"I will leave you soon." Naro said to them. "This beautiful universe is a place for you to play, a place for you to practice the gifts of knowledge and power I will leave with you."

The people watched with wonder as Naro the Younger stood. Streamers of light shimmered from him as he braced his front legs. Placing his still warm feelers open to the sky, he took a long deep breath. Swaying back and forth and forth and back, he sang:

*"Knowledge and power are gifts I give to
you.
Honor them and use them well in all…
you say and do.
The universe — a place to play, a place
to practice your gifts every day.*

*Knowledge and power are gifts I give to you.
Honor them and use them well in
everything you do.
The universe — a place to play, a place
to practice your gifts every day.
Knowledge and power….
Use them well in everything you do."*

When his song was finished,
Naro the Younger lowered his
front legs, but he continued to
sway, back and forth and forth
and back, drumming lightly. In
the hush that followed, he
rubbed his feelers together
once more. Sparks flew.

Light flowed from the Younger Spider's body until he was encircled by a fiery golden glow. The light grew then dimmed, growing fainter and fainter, and fainter.

As the sun began its journey across the morning sky, the Younger Spider vanished, never to be seen on the face of earth again...

...except in dreams.

The Ancient Spider's Eyes

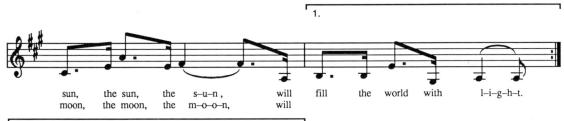